If You Take a Mouse to the Movies

If You Take a Mouse to the Movies

If You Take a

BY Laura Numeroff

ILLUSTRATED BY Felicia Bond

SCHOLASTIC INC.

New York Toronto London Auckland Sydney
Mexico City New Delhi Hong Kong Buenos Aires

Mouse to the Movies

ISBN 0-439-25406-X

Text copyright © 2000 by Laura Numeroff. Illustrations copyright © 2000 by Felicia Bond. All rights reserved. Published by Scholastic Inc., 557 Broadway, New York, NY 10012, by arrangement with HarperCollins Publishers. SCHOLASTIC and associated logos are trademarks and/or registered trademarks of Scholastic Inc.

22 21 20   7 8 9/0

Printed in the U.S.A.   23
First Scholastic printing, November 2002

NOW SHOWING

NOW SHOWING

If you take a mouse to the movies,

he'll ask you for some popcorn.

When you give him the popcorn,

he'll want to string it all together.

Then he'll want to hang it on a Christmas tree.

You'll have to buy him one.

On the way home, he'll see a
snowman in your neighbor's yard.
He'll want to make one of his own.

Then he'll need a carrot for a nose.

When he's all finished, he'll decide to build a fort.
He'll ask you to help him.

Then he'll want to make some snowballs and have a snowball fight.

Playing outside will make him cold.
He'll want to go inside and curl up on the couch.

He'll ask you for a blanket.

Once he's nice and cozy,
he'll want to listen to Christmas carols.

You'll have to find some on the radio.

He'll probably sing along.

The carols will remind him of his Christmas tree,
so he'll want to make ornaments.

You'll get him some paper and glue.

He'll ask you for glitter.

When the ornaments are done,

he'll hang them all up.

Then he'll stand back
to look at the tree.

He'll notice his popcorn string is missing!

So he'll want to make another one.

He'll ask you for some popcorn.

And chances are,
when you give him the popcorn,

he'll want you to take him to the movies.